PINGU

Has a Hard Time

BBC CHILDREN'S BOOKS

PINGU AND THE DOCTOR

One morning Mum had to go to the dentist. Pingu
and Pinga were to stay behind at home on their
own.

"Good luck, Mum," called Pingu as Mum set off.

"Let's play dentists," Pingu said to Pinga. "I'll be
the dentist and you just open your mouth."

Pinga was a good patient and sat quite still while
Pingu poked around in her mouth with a wooden
spoon.

But when Pinga saw Pingu approaching her with
Dad's work tools, she was very alarmed.

"Just a little work to be done," said Pingu
cheerfully.

"No!" Pinga screamed and began to run away.

Pingu chased Pinga round and round the house
until – BUMP – Pingu ran straight into the upturned
table and squashed his beak hard against it.

Poor old Pingu. His beak hurt a lot and was starting to bleed. Pinga wrapped it tightly in a bandage.

"You'll have to go to the doctor," she said.

Pingu and Pinga set off together for the doctor.
There was a big queue outside and everyone
looked very ill and unhappy.

Pinga marched straight up to the doctor. "Help,
help. You've got to help," she cried.

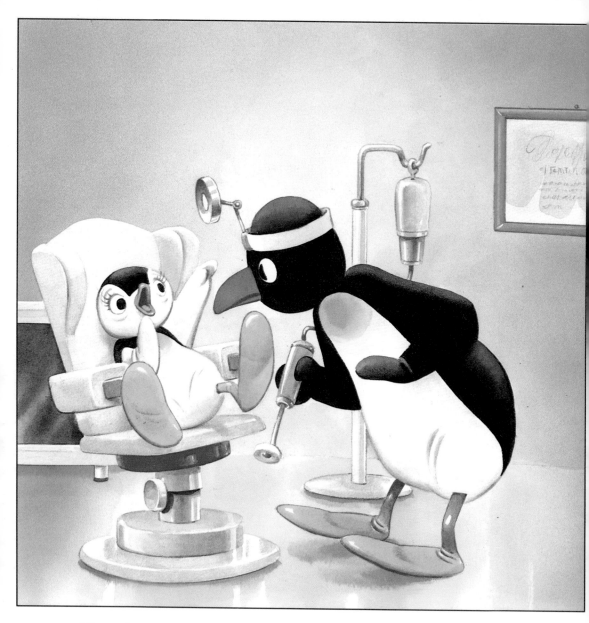

The doctor rushed Pinga inside.

"Now, where does it hurt?" he asked.

"No, no," shrieked Pinga. "I'm all right. It's my brother who's badly hurt his beak. He's outside."

The doctor fetched Pingu in from outside.

He tried to examine Pingu's beak, but Pingu took one look at the doctor's instrument and decided to leave.

"Hey, come back here," cried the doctor.

As the doctor and Pinga rushed outside after him,
Pingu gave them both the slip and tore back into
the doctor's house. Quickly he began to telephone
Mum to ask her to come to his rescue.

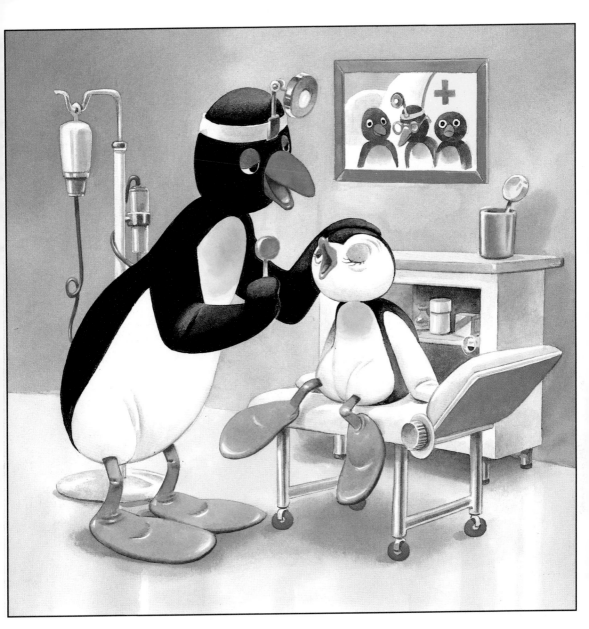

   While they waited for Mum to arrive, the doctor
told Pingu what a brave sister he had.
   "And here's a lollipop for a good little penguin
who opens her mouth nicely for the doctor," he
said.

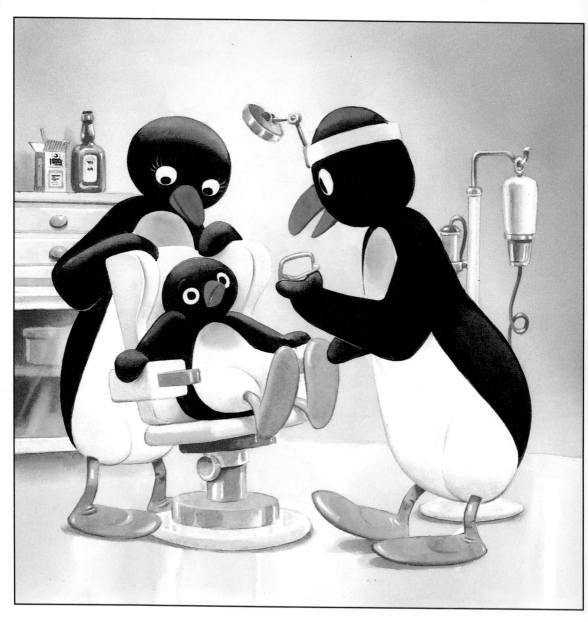

At last Mum arrived and patted Pingu's head
while the doctor looked inside Pingu's beak.

"Only a sprain," the doctor said finally, "but he'll
have to wear a brace on it for a couple of days until
it gets better."

It was time to go home.

"You can look inside my mouth now, if you like," said Pinga.

The doctor smiled. "I don't need to, but here's another lollipop for you instead."

"I've got two lollipops now," said Pinga to Pingu
on the way home. "I could keep one for you, or I
could eat it myself."

"Hmmmmmm," said Pingu.

PINGU AND THE SEAGULL

For his birthday Mum and Dad had given Pingu
a brand new scooter. Today Pingu was taking it
outside for the very first time. He was proud of it
and didn't want to get it dirty.

Just then a seagull came by. It flew over Pingu for
a while and then – SPLAT – some droppings landed
on the new scooter.

Pingu made a large snowball and lobbed it
straight at the seagull.

"Take that!" he shouted.

"Don't be so cross with me," said the seagull.
"You were just unlucky."

Inside his house, Pingu carefully cleaned up the
scooter so that it soon looked spanking new again.
This time he thought it was safer to leave it inside.

The seagull was waiting for him outside.

"Let's play together," it called out to Pingu.
"I know lots of good games."

"No, thanks. I've got better things to do," Pingu
shouted back.

Pingu couldn't believe his eyes. "Wretched bird!
Can't you be more careful?" he shouted and
waved an angry fist at the seagull who was still
circling overhead.

To Pingu's fury the seagull stayed around, flying
over him and jeering at him. At last it stopped for a
drink. As it dipped its beak in the water a lobster
suddenly took hold of it and wouldn't let go.

"You deserve that," said Pingu chuckling. But then
he felt sorry for the trapped seagull and began to
tug as hard as he could at the tail end of the
lobster.

When at last the lobster let go it began to chase
Pingu instead.

"Don't you touch me," cried Pingu, hurrying
through his front door.

Pingu soon came out again, carrying two large
saucepan lids. He banged them together over and
over again, chasing the lobster back into the water.

"Instead of being able to play outside on my own,
I have to keep fighting stupid animals," Pingu
muttered to himself. And just as he was thinking that
– SPLAT – some more seagull droppings landed on
his head!

Pingu was furious. "I do you a good turn and this is what I get in return," he shouted at the seagull.

Mum came out of the house to see what all the noise was about.

"My poor little Pingu," said Mum soothingly as
she scrubbed Pingu clean.

   And as the nice soapy water washed over Pingu's
head he soon began to feel ready for anything
again.

PINGU'S ADMIRER

One morning Pingu was reading his favourite book after breakfast.

"Just look at the time, Pingu," said Mum. "You'll be late for school."

There was a new girl at school today and she
watched Pingu admiringly as he sat at his desk and
arranged his pens. Pingu took no notice of her at all.

"You must be Pingi," said the schoolteacher.
"Welcome to the school."

"Yes, I'm Pingi," said the little penguin quietly.
"I've just moved here."

Pingi needed somewhere to sit. All the pupils
cried out, "Sit at my desk," – except for Pingu. He
spread his things out to take up as much room as
possible. He wasn't going to share his desk with a
girl!

But that's exactly what he had to do. The teacher
placed Pingi next to him! Pingu scowled and
grudgingly moved his things over to make room
for her.

"Psst, Pingi," whispered Pingo from the next desk, "Would you like a lollipop?"

Pingi wasn't interested. She only had eyes for Pingu.

A little later Pingi tapped Pingu and showed him a
heart she had drawn. She gazed at him adoringly.
Pingu was furious. "I've had enough of girls," he
growled.

When it was time to go home, Pingi started to
follow Pingu.

"Get lost," shouted Pingu. "If you have to go the
same way as me you can keep your distance."

Pingi started to cry.

Then Pingi decided to take her revenge. She
hurled a huge snowball at Pingu.

Pingu immediately threw one back at her, but –
oops – it missed and went straight through
someone's window with a loud crash.

The door of the igloo opened and out stomped a very cross penguin.

"Quick," said Pingi. "Let's hide in this barrel."
Pingu leaped in after her only just in time.

Inside the barrel Pingu and Pingi were terrified. They could hear the furious penguin shouting outside. "Where are you, you rascals? I'll catch you and make you pay for my new window."

At last the angry penguin gave up looking for
them.

Pingu and Pingi crept carefully out of the barrel.
Pingu dusted Pingi down and then the penguins
carried on their way together.

At the crossroads they waved goodbye.
"See you tomorrow, Pingi," said Pingu cheerfully.
"Goodbye Pingu," said Pingi, delighted to have
made a new friend.

Published by BBC Books, a division of BBC Enterprises Limited, Woodlands, 80 Wood Lane, London W12 0TT
First published in hardback 1991. Illustrations by Tony Wolf. Original text by Sibylle von Flue.
This edition © BBC Books by arrangement with Dami Editore 1993
PINGU © Editoy A G Bertschikon ZH 1991. ISBN 0 563 40334 9
Printed and bound in Great Britain by Cambus Litho, East Kilbride